Puffin Books

Small Monkey Tales

Small Monkey lived in a big forest. He lived with a lot of
other monkeys, thousands of monkeys, who sat in the trees
chattering to each other. The young monkeys would jump
and play in the branches, and get up to every trick a monkey
knows, and Small Monkey played monkey tricks too. He
chased the little monkeys, and shouted rude names at the big
ones, and he stole honey from his mother's store, and was
spanked for it. He tickled his father's nose as he snoozed in
the sun, so he was smacked again and said he was sorry, but
he did it all again the next day.

Sometimes he did dangerous things, like teasing poor cross
lonely Baboon or wandering in the leopard's path. He stole a
lady's shopping bag from her basket, and one bold bad day
he shouted aloud a very bad word, one that would make the
sky fall down and all the monkeys would be killed. He was a
bold, bad, mischievous little monkey indeed, but all the same
at the end of the day he went back home to sleep, safe and
sound in the same tall tree, as good as a cosy bed and just as
comforting.

This is a classic book for younger children by the popular
author, John Cunliffe, probably best known for his *Postman
Pat* stories. John Cunliffe now lives in Manchester.

John Cunliffe

Small Monkey Tales

Illustrated by Gerry Downes

Puffin Books

PUFFIN BOOKS

Published by the Penguin Group
Penguin Books Ltd, 27 Wrights Lane, London W8 5TZ, England
Penguin Books USA Inc., 375 Hudson Street, New York, New York 10014, USA
Penguin Books Australia Ltd, Ringwood, Victoria, Australia
Penguin Books Canada Ltd, 10 Alcorn Avenue, Toronto, Ontario, Canada M4V 3B2
Penguin Books (NZ) Ltd, 182–190 Wairau Road, Auckland 10, New Zealand

Penguin Books Ltd, Registered Offices: Harmondsworth, Middlesex, England

First published by André Deutsch 1974
Published in Puffin Books 1977
10 9 8 7 6

Printed in England by Clays Ltd, St Ives plc
Filmset in Monophoto Baskerville

Contents

Small Monkey
and the Old Baboon

Small Monkey lived in a big forest.

He lived with a lot of other monkeys; hundreds of monkeys, thousands of monkeys, who sat in the trees chattering to each other. There were Small Monkey's father and mother, of course, then his sisters, and brothers, and cousins, and half-cousins, and

uncles and aunts, nephews and nieces – far
more than he could ever count or remember.
The young monkeys would jump and play
among the branches, running and chasing
and getting up to every trick a monkey
knows. At night, they always came back to
the same tree to sleep, safe from the prowling
creatures of the forest.

*

There was a tree that only had one of the monkey-kind sleeping in it. It was a very tall tree that stood apart from the others, and an old baboon slept in it, all alone. Sometimes a baboon will leave his troop and live in this queer way, all alone, and this was such a one. His fur was ragged and grey, and he had big staring eyes, and if anyone came near his tree he would shout angrily at them, and clash his long yellow teeth. Every day, Small Monkey's mother said to him, 'Now don't go teasing that old baboon. Sure and sure, he'll bite one of you silly little monkeys one of

these days. He could snap a leg off you, easy
as easy.'

But Small Monkey would not listen. It was
fun teasing old Baboon. When a gang of
young monkeys went leaping off through the
trees to Baboon's tree, Small Monkey went
with them. They sat in the trees all round

Baboon's tree, making rude noises at him. Or they saw him on the ground, hunting for food, and followed him in the trees above, pelting him with nuts and twigs and small stones. This couldn't really hurt him, but it made him very angry.

Then some of the more daring monkeys jumped down from the trees and danced towards him, shouting, 'Yah! Silly old Baboon can't catch me! Funny face! Mangy whiskers! Old flea-bag! Can't catch me!'

Nearer and nearer they went, daring each other on. Baboon stood his ground, making fierce faces at them. Then, when he could bear their teasing no longer, he charged, baring his teeth and yelping with anger. The monkeys scattered, scrambling over the grass, leaping into the trees, running for safety. Baboon was too old to catch them. They got away, as always, and sat in the trees again, making silly noises at him. Though he went away and hid, he could not get away from their silly din. There was no rest or peace for the poor old Baboon, until the young monkeys grew tired of their game. Then one of them thought of a new game to play, and they went whooping off through the forest, leaving Baboon to growl and grumble to himself.

One time, a monkey was too slow, and Baboon gave him a nasty bite. Another time, he bit a good piece off the end of a cheeky monkey's tail, that made the monkey yelp and cry with pain for many a day. It made no difference. They still played their game of teasing old Baboon. When the little monkeys came home, Small Monkey's mother would say, 'Have you been teasing that old Baboon again? You bad little monkey.'

And she would give him a hard smack with her paw, but he would do it again the next day. Poor old Baboon led a sad and lonely life, and none would be his friend. Until, one day, a leopard came prowling through the

forest. He sprang unseen into a tree, and lay quietly on a branch, hidden among the leaves. He looked down on a forest track, waiting for an animal to come along. Then he would drop down upon it, catch it easily, and eat it up. So there the leopard lay, patiently waiting; and all about him in the forest, the little monkeys hunted for their food, not knowing the fierce leopard was so near. Some were in the trees, some down on the ground, searching for fruits and nuts and sweet leaves. Sometimes the monkeys came near, and the leopard's eyes gleamed at the prospect of a good dinner; but they never came quite near enough, or some feeling of danger made them move away again, and

still the leopard waited. Then, at last, he saw a monkey coming straight towards him. It was sniffing eagerly at something, and it trotted along the path that led directly under the leopard's branch. Nearer and nearer it came. It was Small Monkey. Look out, Small Monkey! Oh, look out, or the leopard will get you! But Small Monkey did not look out for danger, as his mother had so often told him to. He was too busy following the lovely scent that tickled his nose. On he came, closer and closer to the leopard. The leopard tensed his muscles ready to spring, waiting for just the right moment. Small Monkey came on.

'Now,' thought the leopard, gathering himself to spring, and ... a terrible screeching filled the forest, making the leopard freeze where he was. Small Monkey, too, stopped and crouched on the path, trembling with fear. Then something big came crashing through the tree. There was a din of the fearful screeching, and angry gnashing of teeth, and a storm seemed to fall upon the leopard. The branches of the trees thrashed about

wildly, and a heavy stick crashed down hard
on his back. The leopard didn't wait to see
what was attacking him, he leapt from the
tree. When Small Monkey saw the leopard,
he cried out in fear. Surely it would kill him,
and eat him up. But the leopard didn't look
at Small Monkey. It ran away, away into the
forest. Something was chasing the leopard,
something that made a dreadful noise and
came crashing through the tree like a
hundred elephants. A great hairy shape
jumped out of the tree, all whirling arms and
legs, and ran after the leopard. It hurled

great branches after the leopard, and uttered shuddering screams of anger that made the leopard run still faster.

When the leopard had gone, the screaming creature quieted itself and turned back to Small Monkey, who still sat trembling on the path. But Small Monkey was astonished. Who was it that had saved him from the leopard? It was old Baboon! Yes, old Baboon himself! Baboon looked at Small Monkey.

'Leopard nearly had you that time, little fellow,' he said. 'Lucky for you there was a silly old Baboon sitting in that tree, that cares nothing for any leopard.'

'Not silly,' said Small Monkey. 'Brave. Brave Baboon. Thank you. Wait.'

Then Small Monkey ran up the stem of a banana plant, which Baboon was too heavy to climb. He broke off a large bunch of bananas, and brought them down and laid them at Baboon's feet. Baboon broke a banana off, and gave it to Small Monkey. Then he took one for himself. So the two of them sat together, eating bananas and talking, and the monkeys in the trees all around looked on, astonished.

From that day onwards, Small Monkey and Baboon were good friends. They often sat together to share a bunch of bananas. In time, the other monkeys of the forest made friends with old Baboon, too, and he was no longer lonely. No one would think of teasing him now. As for the leopard, he never came into that part of the forest again.

Run, Monkey, Run!

Small Monkey sat in a tree.

The tree was near the houses, on the edge of the town.

Small Monkey looked down through the branches. He could see a white gate, and a

path, and bright flowers, and green grass.
Some days, a little boy came along the path
and threw a nice tit-bit to Small Monkey; an
apple-core, or a piece of chocolate, or, best of
all, a sugar-lump.

Small Monkey sat in the tree and waited
for the little boy to come. All the hot afternoon he waited. The shadows moved across
the grass. Small Monkey felt so hungry; but

the little boy did not come. No one came. They were all asleep, in their houses, in the hot hot afternoon.

Small Monkey chirruped a little to himself, and said he would go home. Just then, quick footsteps tap-tapped along the footpath. Small Monkey saw a big woman in a white dress, with a basket on her arm. She stopped at the gate, opened it, and called towards the house, 'Yoo-hoo! Lucy! Are you there?'

There was no answer.

'Oh, drat it, the girl's asleep,' said the woman to herself. She set the basket down on the path, and ran towards the house. Small Monkey looked down into the basket. It was full of good things to eat! There was a crusty loaf of bread, a big fruit pie, a whole bar of chocolate, a bag of sugar, and a strange black thing, with a hard shiny stalk. What a lot of presents for Small Monkey!

He jumped down from his tree. He took hold of the basket's handle. It was too heavy. He could not lift it. So he dipped his paw into the basket, and scooped out the middle of the

pie. He crammed the sweet fruit into his mouth, and the juice ran all over his face, making him sticky. Then he pulled the bread out, and nibbled the end of it. When he was tired of that, he threw it in the flower-bed. He was just tearing the paper from the chocolate, when a voice shouted, 'My shopping! Oh! A monkey's got my shopping! Oh, you nasty beast, put it down!'

It was the big woman, and she came running down the path. Small Monkey dropped the chocolate, but snatched up the sugar and the black thing, and jumped quickly into his tree. He climbed high among the branches, where the woman couldn't reach him. Her face was red now, and she stood looking up at him, shouting, 'Bad monkey. Give it back!'

Small Monkey tore open the bag of sugar, and nuzzled his mouth into it. Then he tipped the bag upside down. The sugar fell

into the woman's face. It went in her eyes. It made her eyebrows and hair white. It went down inside her dress, tickling her. It went inside her ears and nose and mouth. She spluttered and coughed; she shook her head; she shook her whole self. The sugar prickled her all over. She shouted and shouted, but Small Monkey took no notice. He held the queer black thing in his paws, and nibbled at it. It had a strong leathery skin and a funny smell. When he shook it, it jingled. What a silly fruit it was! Small Monkey had never seen such a thing before.

'He's got my purse!' the woman shouted. 'My purse! Help! Throw it down, you bad monkey, you cannot eat that.'

But Small Monkey sat on his branch and held the black thing tightly.

'Just wait till I catch you,' said the woman. Then she went away. Small Monkey nibbled

at the purse again, but he couldn't bite through its skin.

Soon, the woman came back, and there was another woman with her. They carried a ladder between them. They put it against the tree, and the big woman came climbing up towards Small Monkey. Now she seemed bigger than ever! She reached nearer and nearer to Small Monkey, and he sat on his branch, all huddled up with fear. Then, just as the woman stretched out her hand to grab him, Small Monkey jumped. He jumped over the woman's head, then down through the tree, down the ladder to the ground.

'Where has he gone?' said the woman, still looking up into the tree.

Small Monkey ran up the path. The other woman bent down to catch him. He ran between her legs, making her yelp. On went Small Monkey, still holding the purse. Where could he run? The house door stood open. Small Monkey ran into the house, scuttering from room to room. He found a quiet corner, and sat down to nibble and bite and tug at the purse. He tried and tried to open it. It *must* have something good to eat inside.

Then, the house was full of voices. The deep voices of men, mixing with the excited chattering of the women.

'Where is he? We'll soon catch him,' said a loud voice.

Then the room was filled with stamping feet, and Small Monkey crouched in his corner. Where could he run? He pressed back against the wall. He turned his head from side to side, seeking a way out. He still held the purse tightly.

'Now, my little thief. Now I have you,' said a thumping big man. 'Now . . .'

And he bent down, closing his thick hands round Small Monkey. Just then, Small Monkey jumped. He jumped past the man's hands and between his legs. Another two men tried to grab him. He was too quick for them. He ran behind a big chair. They began pulling the chair away from the wall, but Small

Monkey ran to the fireplace. There was a rapid scrabbling, a cloud of soot blew into the room, and Small Monkey was gone.

'Where is he?' said the thick man.

A scratching came from the chimney, that grew fainter and fainter.

'Up the chimney,' said the big woman, 'and he's still got my purse.'

A little while later, a dirty black face poked out of a chimney-pot, and Small Monkey climbed out on to the roof of the house. He was covered in soot! But he still held the purse, and he sat there, chewing at it; turning it round; shaking it; smelling it; looking at it. All this time, the people were banging about with ladders at the side of the house, but Small Monkey took no notice. All he wanted was to open this queer fruit. He would bite it open, and find the good parts to eat inside it. Just as the big man's head came into sight at the edge of the roof, Small Monkey pressed the purse's catch with his paw, not knowing what he had done. The purse flew open. Small Monkey scooped his paw into it, and brought out three hard round things, very shiny, with shapes made on them. Small Monkey crammed them into his mouth. Oh, what a nasty surprise he had! He pulled a face, and spat the things out, for they hurt his teeth and tasted most horrid. They rolled down the roof, and bounced into the garden.

'My money!' the big woman shouted from below.

Small Monkey scooped his paw in again. He only found some pieces of paper with pictures and funny shapes on them. He let the wind take them, and blow them far away

across the garden. The women ran after them, calling and squealing to each other. Then Small Monkey clashed his teeth angrily, and threw the empty purse at the man's head. He ran across the roof, and jumped into a tree, and from there to another tree, swinging and leaping away into the great forest that was his home.

Monkey's Wonderful Box

One day, Small Monkey found such a strange thing.

A queer glittery thing it was, lying in the grass under a banana plant. Small Monkey walked all round it. He looked at it this way. He looked at it that way. He could not tell what it was.

Sniff. Sniff.

Small Monkey sniffed the air. He could

only smell bananas and grass. Small Monkcy
sat down and watched the thing; for ten minutes . . . for twenty minutes. The thing did
not move – not once.

'What is it?' he said to himself.

Then he became angry, and snapped his
teeth at the thing.

Still it did not move.

It was not afraid of Small Monkey.

Small Monkey turned away.

'Silly,' said Small Monkey. 'Won't run away. Won't fight. No smell. Won't talk. Silly thing.'

But he turned back to it, all the same. He could not leave it lying there, teasing him. Small Monkey crept closer to the thing. What if it should be a trap?

'Too little for a trap,' said Small Monkey. 'Not banana. Not coconut. Wrong shape. Wrong colour. All shiny. Good to eat?'

Small Monkey stretched out one finger, nearer and nearer to the thing. Then . . . he touched its very edge, and jumped up and ran away, chattering his teeth. Still the thing did not move. Small Monkey crept back again, feeling more brave. The funny thing lay quietly in the grass. Suddenly, Small Monkey jumped on the thing, and held it down, and bit it!

The thing did not squeal. No juice came out of it. And oh, how it hurt Small Monkey's teeth! He threw it down on the ground. There was a *click*, and the thing sprang open, like a shell. It was a little box, with a lid.

What could be in it? Small Monkey looked inside it, putting his face close.

'Pretty!' he said. 'Pretty, pretty, pretty!'

Small Monkey had never seen anything so pretty. He jumped high into the air, chittering and laughing to himself. He danced all round the little box. Then he stopped, and looked again. Closer and closer he put his face. He gazed and gazed at the lovely thing inside it. Then he took it in his hands. It closed with a *snap*. Oh . . . the pretty thing was gone! Again, Small Monkey threw the box on the ground. Again, it sprang open. Again, he could see the pretty thing inside it. Small

Monkey was full of joy. He closed the box.
He threw it down, and it opened again, and
there was the pretty thing again, inside it. He
could find it whenever he wished!

*

'Monkey's treasure,' said Small Monkey. 'Must show elephant.' So off he went to the river bank, to show elephant his treasure.

'See what I have,' said Small Monkey. 'See

my treasure.' And he threw the box down on the ground in front of elephant, so that it sprang open.

'Look in it,' he said. 'Look close. Won't bite. Pretty.'

Elephant bent his great head down, curling up his trunk, and looked into the strange box.

'Oh! Oh!' cried elephant. 'There's a great big poisonous snake in it, waiting to strike! You bad little monkey, to play such a trick.' He trumpeted angrily, and threw the box down, and stamped off into the jungle.

Small Monkey was sad. Why was elephant so cross with him? Fearfully, he picked his box up, and looked inside it. *Was* there a snake in it?

'No,' said Small Monkey. 'No snake in monkey's box. Pretty thing. Pretty thing. Why did elephant say there was a snake?'

Small Monkey was so puzzled. Whenever *he* looked in his box he saw a pretty creature, smiling at him.

*

Just then, a vulture flew down. It looked at Small Monkey's shining box.

'What you got there?' asked vulture, rudely.

'A pretty box,' said Small Monkey.

'I can see that,' said vulture, 'but what's in it? Any dead meat?'

'No,' said Small Monkey. 'Pretty thing. Look!'

Vulture looked in the box.

'Ugh!' he said. 'Nasty. You call that pretty? Looks too nasty even for me to eat, and I'm not fussy. Ugh! Nasty. Nasty. Nasty. Horrid little monkey, to play such a trick!'

Vulture glared fiercely at Small Monkey,

and flew away. Small Monkey looked in his box. There was the pretty thing, as before.

'Why did vulture say monkey's box was nasty?' he said sadly.

Small Monkey closed his box, and walked along through the jungle until he met hyena. Hyena was just finishing his dinner, so it was safe to stop and talk to him.

'See my pretty box?' said Small Monkey.

'Yes,' said hyena, 'but what's in it? Anything funny?'

'Not funny,' said Small Monkey. 'Pretty. Look.'

So hyena looked in monkey's box.

Suddenly, hyena began to laugh.

'Haw! Haw! Haw! Hooooooooooo! Haw! Haw!' Yowling and braying, hyena's laughter echoed through the jungle, striking terror into animals for miles around.

'Not funny. Not funny,' said Small Monkey, almost in tears. 'Give it back.'

'Oh dear, oh dear, it's the funniest thing I ever saw,' said hyena. 'What a face! Oh dear! Oh deary me.'

Small Monkey took his box, and closed it firmly, and hurried away before hyena began his terrible laughing again.

'Pretty thing,' he said, tearfully. And all the rest of the day he would not open his box. He met antelope, and gibbon, and parakeet, and giraffe, and rhinoceros; they all asked him to open his box, but all he would say was, 'No. Monkey's secret. Only for monkey to look in.'

That night, when it was quite dark, and

Small Monkey was alone, then he did open his box. He looked in it.

'Oh. Oh. Oh,' cried Small Monkey. 'It's gone! Monkey's pretty thing has gone!'

It was true. There was no pretty thing. It had gone. There was nothing. Small Monkey began to wail and weep, and soon someone heard him and called up to him in the darkness, 'Hi there, Small Monkey! What's

the matter? Has a tiger bitten your tail off?'

It was old Baboon who lived near by, and Small Monkey soon dried his tears and hopped down and told Baboon the whole story, for he was a good friend to Small Monkey.

'May I see the box?' asked Baboon.

Small Monkey handed it to him. Baboon held the open box up to the light of the moon that had just come out, and looked into it. When he saw what he saw, he smiled to himself.

'Can *you* tell where my pretty thing has gone?' said Small Monkey, anxiously.

'Yes, dear little monkey,' said Baboon, kindly. 'You will see your pretty thing when the sun shines in the sky again tomorrow. And do you know what your pretty thing is?'

'I cannot tell,' said Small Monkey. 'Do you know? Is it a magic box? For elephant saw a snake in it; and vulture saw a nasty thing in it; and hyena saw a funny thing in it.'

'No, not magic,' said Baboon, laughing. 'It

has a thing in it that men make. A thing called a mirror.'

'Mirror?' said Small Monkey.

'Yes. A mirror,' said Baboon. 'When you look at it you see your own face.'

'My *own* face?' said Small Monkey.

'Yes,' said Baboon, 'and *that* is your pretty thing. Your very own face!'

'My very own face!' exclaimed Small Monkey, hugging himself in glee. 'And the others...?'

'Elephant saw his trunk, and thought it was a snake,' said Baboon. 'Vulture saw his very own nasty face. Hyena saw his very own funny face.'

'Oh! Oh! What a joke,' said Small Monkey. The two of them laughed and laughed and laughed, in the dark night. They smiled and chuckled together over it, and talked of all the animals they would show the wonderful box to, and what they would say when they looked in it, until it was time to go to sleep.

Small Monkey's Naughty Day

Small Monkey was often naughty. He knew all the tricks and mischiefs that so delight the monkey-kind. He chased the little monkeys, pulling their tails and tweaking their ears when he caught them. He shouted rude names at the big monkeys, and ran so fast that they could never catch him. He stole honey from his mother's store, and was spanked for it. He tickled his father's nose with a blade of grass, as he snoozed in the hot sun, making him sneeze and waken up. He was smacked again, said he was sorry, and did it all again the next day. There was no curing him. He was a true monkey.

One day, he was naughtier than he had ever been before. He had played all his tricks. He had been smacked four times. Now he sat in his tree, wondering what to do next. He wanted to be still naughtier. He wanted to do something new, something really bad. What could he do? He thought and thought. He couldn't think of any new tricks, and he had grown tired of the old ones. Oh, *what* could he do? His eyes darted about, looking for mischief to be done, but seeing none. Then he remembered something an old monkey had once told him. It was a word; a very very bad word, that must never be spoken aloud. The

old monkey had whispered it into his ear, and Small Monkey, being quite little at the time, had shaken with fear. The old monkey had said that if this word, this bad bad word, should be spoken aloud, then the sky would fall down and all the monkeys would be killed. No one must ever say it aloud, it was so evil and full of bad magic. Then he had whispered the word in Small Monkey's ear:

'Raccaramba. Raccaramba.'

Small Monkey's legs had gone wobbly with fright, and he had run away from the old monkey, so that he would not hear the bad word again. He had cuddled close up to his mother, and covered his ears with his paws, so frightened he was.

*

Now Small Monkey had grown up to be strong and bold. He was not afraid of a little thing like a word, now. This would be his new naughtiness. He would say it. He would say the bad word out loud. Better – he would shout it. He would shout it to the sky. Would the sky dare to fall? No. Small Monkey was not afraid. The sky would never fall. He was strong, and afraid of nothing.

When the other monkeys heard what Small Monkey was up to, they began to chatter in great excitement. Some said, 'Stop him! Stop him!'

Others said, 'He'll never dare do it. Don't be afraid.'

Some hid their faces in their paws, too frightened to look. Some rolled about in the grass, laughing at Small Monkey's silliness. But Small Monkey took no notice of any of them. He began to climb up and up into the tallest tree; he said he must climb as near to the sky as he could. Up he went; up and up, until he was perched on the highest branch

that would hold him. He swayed about as the wind blew; almost in the clouds, it seemed to those below. The older monkeys took no notice.

'Up to some foolery, again,' they muttered, and went on feeding. But the little monkeys were hopping with glee and fear. Would he do it? Would he dare?

Small Monkey looked up into the sky. He opened his mouth and shouted, 'Racca . . . ! Racca . . . !'

He was too nervous to say the whole word, and his shout was like a shouted whisper. Then, he tried again. This time he shouted as

loudly as he could, 'RACCA...! RACCA...!
RACCARAMBA!'

He had done it! He clung to the branch,
with his eyes shut tightly, waiting for the sky
to fall. He opened his eyes. The sky was just
the same. He tried again.

'RACCARAMBA! RACCARAMBA!'

Nothing happened. Nothing! He kept his
eyes open, and the sky didn't even shake.
Now Small Monkey was satisfied. He had
dared to do what was forbidden. He had
been naughtier than ever before. He climbed

down the tree. All the little monkeys danced round him, when he reached the ground. They cheered him, and admired him. What a brave little monkey he was. Some said he would be king of the monkeys one day. They all wanted to be friends with him, brought

him presents and made him the leader in all
their games. How proud Small Monkey was.
He was the monkey who dared.

The little monkeys were so busy playing that
they didn't notice black storm clouds piling
up across the sky. The forest grew dark, and
their mothers called them to come and shel-
ter. As the big rain-drops began to fall, the
little monkeys scurried to their mothers, and
pressed close to their warm fur. Small

Monkey had seen rain-storms before, and knew it would soon pass away.

Then something happened that he hadn't seen before. There was an enormous banging roar, and a bright crack ran across the sky. Small Monkey gazed in terror. There was another rolling bang, and another brilliant crack split the sky across. Small Monkey

began to tremble with fear. Surely, the sky was breaking, and soon it would fall down and kill them all! Small Monkey began to cry, and buried his face in his mother's fur.

'Don't be afraid,' said his mother, holding him close, 'it's only a thunderstorm. It won't hurt you.'

But nothing would stop Small Monkey crying, and shaking with fear. The thunder banged across the sky again and again, and the lightning crackled across the sky. Small Monkey was sure the world was ending.

'It's all my fault! It's all my fault!' he wailed.

'No, no, how can a thunderstorm be your fault? What a silly little monkey you are,' said his mother.

Small Monkey pressed close to his mother, and closed his eyes, and held his paws over his ears, but still he could not keep the thunder noise out. He had never in his life been so afraid. He should not have shouted that bad word at the sky. His naughtiness had gone too far this time. There was a bigger and closer noise; a great tearing and crashing, that came down upon them. His mother jumped for her life, with Small Monkey clinging to her. Now, at last, he thought, the sky really was falling. One piece had just missed them. The next one would surely get them. He waited for it to come. Nothing came. The storm was dying away. The thunder quietened; and lightning flashed gently, now, far away at the edge of the sky. The storm passed away. The sun came out again. Small Monkey opened his eyes. The sky was still in its place. It had not fallen after all. Small Monkey *was* surprised. But something had fallen; a big tree, that had been struck by lightning. It had fallen very near, but by good luck it had not hurt any of the monkeys.

Small Monkey dried his tears. He smoothed his fur, and whisked his tail. All was well, after all. But he would never never say that bad word again. Never. He left his mother, and went to play with the other little monkeys again. But they wouldn't play with him! They scowled at him, and shouted, 'It was all your fault. You nearly made the sky fall. See, that tree fell anyway. Go away, Small Monkey! Go away!'

Then they pelted him with nuts and berries, and Small Monkey had to run away and hide. Later, he went to tell his friend old Baboon all that had happened. Old Baboon listened solemnly to Small Monkey's story. Then he said, 'So it was you that made that nasty storm come, was it?'

'Yes,' said Small Monkey.

'And it was you that made the sky crack, and almost fall?'

'Yes.'

'Oh, Small Monkey, you are a funny one. Oh, oh, deary me...' said old Baboon, beginning to laugh. Then he rolled on the ground, and hugged himself, and snorted with laughter.

'There's nothing funny,' said Small Monkey.

'Oh yes there is,' said old Baboon.

'What?'

'*You.*'

Then Small Monkey looked sad, and old Baboon felt sorry for him, and said, 'Don't be sad, Small Monkey. You didn't make the storm with your bad word.'

'Didn't I?'

'No. It was a thunderstorm. It grew in the sky by itself. No one could make it. No one could stop it.'

'And didn't the sky crack?' said Small Monkey, beginning to smile.

'No. The sky cannot crack. That was

lightning. But it did hit that old tree, and make it fall down.'

'I didn't do it?'

'No. You only said a word. That didn't do anything.'

'Are you sure?'

'Yes.'

'Sure?'

'Yes.'

'Quite sure?'

'Yes. I'm sure I'm sure. Sure as sure can ever be.'

'Hurrah!' shouted Small Monkey.

He was happy again.

Small Monkey was never afraid of thunderstorms after that. As for that bad word – he never said it again; just in case . . .

Small Monkey
and the Cheetahs

When it was time to go to sleep, all the monkeys climbed up and up, into the high branches of their tree. Then they climbed out along the slender branches, until they found a good place to curl up, safe from the hunting beasts of the forest. Their day-long chattering died away; sleep and silence came upon them.

*

One quiet dusk, a cheetah came prowling by
their tree. She could not find the antelope she
usually hunted. She thought she would have
a fat little monkey for her supper instead. So
she jumped softly into the monkeys' tree, and
began to climb, silent as a shadow. When she
came to Small Monkey's branch she paused.
She had seen him. A nice little monkey; just
right for her supper. She stepped upon his
branch. It was not a thick branch. Gently
Cheetah stepped; oh, so gently; but gentle,
and soft, and slow as she was, the branch
trembled a little under her weight. Cheetah

crept slowly along the branch, stalking Small
Monkey: nearer and nearer. Small Monkey
was deep in his dreams. Cheetah came
nearer, her sharp teeth catching the moon's
light. Her red tongue licked about her nose;
how hungry she was! Nearer. Still Small
Monkey did not awake. Nearer came
Cheetah, testing each step, moving with
endless care; the smallest sound would waken
Small Monkey, she knew. But the branch was
beginning to bend under Cheetah's weight,
and all her care could not stop it. The more
she moved along it, the more it bent. She laid
her ears back in anger. The branch dipped
under her, but still she moved along it – she
could not stop, she must catch Small Monkey
no matter how much the branch should

bend! The branch dipped and swayed dangerously. Now it shook under Cheetah, and its shaking wakened Small Monkey. For a moment he stared at Cheetah. Then he jumped! He jumped away through the tree,

branch to branch, chattering with anger. The branch Cheetah was on shook still more, and she clung to it for her life. Now the other monkeys awoke, and pelted Cheetah with nuts and berries, and she climbed down the tree as fast as she could, and ran away.

The clever monkeys always slept on thin

branches, so that no big creature could catch them, as Cheetah had found out. But Cheetah was so angry that she said she would find a way to catch Small Monkey, in spite of this.

A few nights later, Cheetah came to Small Monkey's tree again. She didn't come alone.

A second cheetah followed close behind her; a little cheetah, only a quarter the size of the first one. Cheetah had brought her young son to help her to catch Small Monkey. It would be a good lesson for him, in hunting. She sent Little Cheetah up the tree, and waited and watched on the ground below.

*

Little Cheetah climbed until he found Small
Monkey's branch. He knew Small Monkey
by the markings on his fur. He stepped on to
the branch, quietly and gently. The branch
was thin, but Little Cheetah was light on his
paws, only a quarter the weight of his
mother. Little Cheetah crept out along the
branch, and it held his weight without bending or trembling. He would catch Small
Monkey, and eat him. Small Monkey slept at
the end of his branch, not dreaming that
Little Cheetah was coming softly to get him,
nearer and nearer, without bending his slender branch. But Small Monkey had chosen a
different branch tonight. It was one that
stretched out over the deep river. Little
Cheetah hated climbing out over the dark

water; his mother had not taught him to
swim, and he feared the water. Even so, he
stalked along the branch over the water, for
his mother would beat him hard if he showed
fear, or if he failed to get Small Monkey.
Now he was a long way along the branch;
light as he was, the branch began to dip and
dip under him, and seemed to tip him nearer
to the black water. Little Cheetah was frightened. But now he could almost reach Small
Monkey. He would hold him in his sharp
claws, and run back, away from the water, to
safety. Then he would have this fat little
monkey for his supper, sharing it with his
mother. He licked his lips. He stretched out
his paw to grasp Small Monkey. Then, Small
Monkey awoke! There was Little Cheetah's
fierce face, so near to him. There was the

cruel paw, just ready to plunge its claws into him. How frightened Small Monkey was! How could he get away? He could not jump to another branch; Little Cheetah was too near for that. He could not run; there was nowhere to run to. There was no time to think; in a moment Little Cheetah would have him. Little Cheetah edged still nearer, then brought his paw down to hold Small Monkey. The branch shook. His paw hit the branch, not soft fur as he expected. He scrabbled about in the darkness with two paws now, trying to find Small Monkey. He wasn't there! There was a *plip* in the water below. Now the branch waved about wildly. Little Cheetah was so busy fighting the darkness, striking about with his claws, trying to catch Small Monkey, that he lost his own hold on the branch. Now there was a loud *plop* in the water. Waiting below, mother

Cheetah could not tell what was happening. She had heard the branch shaking. Then a little splash, followed by a bigger splash. What *was* her son up to? Then she saw him. He was in the river! He was floundering in the deep water. A minute more, and he would be swept away by the current and drowned! She dived into the water, and caught her son by the neck, holding him in her mouth as though he were a cub again. So she swam to the bank with him, and dropped him on the grass. He was a sad sight. His coat was draggled and dirty, and he was shivering

with fear. Even so, his mother smacked him. She cuffed him with her heavy paw, because he had let Small Monkey get away again. She growled deep in her throat, and said he must come again to catch Small Monkey. There was no sign of Small Monkey now, so she took him off home to bed, without any supper.

Small Monkey was quite safe. He was some way away, drying himself in the long grass. He knew how lucky he was. His mother had taught him to dive and swim, for the monkeys often caught shellfish under the water. So, when Little Cheetah tried to get him, Small Monkey simply let go of his branch, and dropped into the river. Then he swam under water until he was a good way down river, where the cheetahs couldn't see or smell him. He crept out of the water, and hid until he was sure that the cheetahs had gone away. Then he climbed back into his tree, to a very high branch, curled up, and went to sleep.

*

The cheetahs came back the next night.

Again mother Cheetah waited on the ground, whilst Little Cheetah climbed up into the tree. This time, Small Monkey was sleeping on a very thin branch at the top of the tree. Little Cheetah had to climb very high to find him. When he crept out along the branch, the ground seemed very far away. The branch was so thin that it shook, even under Little Cheetah's small weight. Still he crept along it; he knew that his mother would be very angry if he didn't catch Small Monkey this time, and he would go to bed again without any supper. Nearer and nearer he came to Small Monkey. Where *had* he gone to, last night? Little Cheetah could not guess, but he was glad there was no water under him this time. Nearer . . . nearer; now the branch was shaking and bending more and more, it was so thin. This wakened Small Monkey, but he pretended to be asleep. He watched Little Cheetah through one just-open eye. He waited until he was a good way along the branch. Then, he began to swing the branch up and down, up and down. Now Little Cheetah could see that Small Monkey was awake, but what was he doing? He stared at Small Monkey, and held on to the branch in terror. He could not move, the branch was swaying about so dangerously; he clung on with all four paws, pressing himself close to the branch, not daring to go forward or backward. But Small Monkey swung the branch more and more; up and down it went, lashing about as though in a storm. Little Cheetah felt himself being shaken loose. He began to feel dizzy. He howled for Small Monkey to stop. But Small Monkey would not stop. Still more he

swung at the branch, gripping it tightly with
his clever monkey-paws. Up and down, up
and down, it went, more and more wildly.
All the tree seemed to whirl round and round
poor Little Cheetah, and, just when he felt he
could hold on no longer, there was a loud
crackling noise! The branch had broken.
Small Monkey jumped at once to another
branch. The broken branch, with Little
Cheetah still clinging to it, went crashing
down through the tree. The tree's other
branches whipped and lashed Little Cheetah

as he fell through the tree. He could well
have been killed when he struck the ground,
but his fall was softened by mother Cheetah;
he fell right on top of her! She didn't know
what had hit her, and began to run for her

life. When she saw she was not being chased by a lion or a tiger, she came slowly back to the tree. There lay her son and a sorry sight he was. Bruised, and torn, and bleeding, he lay limply waiting for her. There was no sign of Small Monkey. She growled and lashed her tail, but she hadn't the heart to smack her son this time. She licked his wounds, and carried him gently home.

Small Monkey was safe in his tree. He knew he had beaten the cheetahs. They never came back again; but Small Monkey was always careful to choose the thinnest possible branch, when he curled up to go to sleep.

Also in Young Puffin

The
Reluctant Dragon

Kenneth Grahame

"Don't you worry. It's only a dragon."

Dragons are supposed to be huge, fiery
monsters chasing knights and devouring
small children. But the Boy knows more
about dragons than anyone else because
he's read about them. So he's not worried
when a real dragon moves into a cave up
on the Downs. This dragon is more
interested in reciting poetry and just
wants a quiet life. But peace and quiet is
hard to find – especially when St George
the dragon-slayer turns up to fight!

Also in Young Puffin

THE
LITTLE WITCH

Margaret Mahy

**Some stories are true, and some
aren't...**

Six surprising tales about sailors and
pirates, witches and witch-babies,
orphans and children, and even lions and
dragons!

Also in Young Puffin

Rat Saturday

Margaret Nash

**"Go on, Joe, I dare you to go
to Teabag's."
"Right!" said Joe, suddenly feeling
brave. "I jolly well will go!"**

Does 'Old Teabag' really live in a damp
cellar with rats running up his legs? Joe
decides to find out. Imagine his surprise
when he meets two very friendly, very
tame pet rats! It's not long before Joe
and his friend Donna discover that tame
rats can be a lot of fun!

Also in Young Puffin

Brinsly's Dream

Petronella Breinburg

"Football, football, that's all you can think of," said Brinsly's sister.

And she was right. Brinsly just lived for football. He knew his team would have to practise really hard if they were going to win a few matches – and maybe even win the festival trophy!

CHRIS and the DRAGON

Fay Sampson

Chris Chudley is never out of trouble!

Chris just can't help getting into mischief
– even when he decides to try extra hard
to be good! Starting with an exploding
dragon in a Christmas display and ending
with another kind of dragon – Mrs
Maltby the headmistress! – Chris's
exploits around town and at school make
hilarious reading.